THE
Artful
GODDAUGHTER

THE
Artful
GODDAUGHTER

MELODIE CAMPBELL

RAVEN BOOKS
an imprint of
ORCA BOOK PUBLISHERS

Library and Archives Canada Cataloguing in Publication

Campbell, Melodie, 1955-, author
The artful goddaughter/ Melodie Campbell.
(Rapid reads)

Issued also in print and electronic formats.
ISBN 978-1-4598-0819-5 (pbk.).--ISBN 978-1-4598-0820-1 (pdf).--
ISBN 978-1-4598-0821-8 (epub)

I. Title. II. Series: Rapid reads
PS8605.A54745A77 2014   C813'.6   C2014-901567-4
C2014-901568-2

First published in the United States, 2014
Library of Congress Control Number: 2014935364

Summary: In this work of crime fiction, Gina Gallo, mob goddaughter and
unwilling sleuth, tries to return a valuable painting to the art gallery. (RL 3.5)

*Orca Book Publishers is dedicated to preserving the environment and has
printed this book on Forest Stewardship Council® certified paper.*

Orca Book Publishers gratefully acknowledges the support for
its publishing programs provided by the following agencies:
the Government of Canada through the Canada Book Fund and the
Canada Council for the Arts, and the Province of British Columbia
through the BC Arts Council and the Book Publishing Tax Credit.

Cover design by Jenn Playford
Cover photography by Shutterstock

ORCA BOOK PUBLISHERS   ORCA BOOK PUBLISHERS
PO Box 5626, Stn. B   PO Box 468
Victoria, BC Canada   Custer, WA USA
V8R 6S4   98240-0468

www.orcabook.com
Printed and bound in Canada.

17 16 15 14 • 4 3 2 1

For Natalie and Alex,
my smart and witty daughters.

ONE

When I was a girl, my favorite movie was *The Pink Panther*.

Great-Uncle Franco owned a movie theater in town. He had a knock-off reel. We'd beg him to play that film on the big screen. I probably saw it thirty times. It became an obsession with me.

When other girls dressed up for Halloween as princesses, I was decked out in head-to-toe black. With a mask.

"Girls can't be cat burglars," my cousin Paulo told me.

"Yeah?" I yelled back. "What about Mad Magda?"

Paulo sneered. "She's not real. She's just a legend, like Santa Claus. Only boys are burglars."

This obviously did some serious damage. Because, of course, I had to prove him wrong. Even if it took me twenty years to do it.

My name is Gina Gallo. That's what it says on my passport—or at least one of them.

I'm a gemologist by trade, not a professional cat burglar. The last thing I want now is a life of crime. But I am known in this burg for some pretty daring escapades. Some were even successful. Others, not so much.

My fiancé, Pete, would say, "You're still out of jail. That's successful."

Frankly, I'd call it a miracle. Especially since I was now contemplating murder.

It had happened again, and I was ready to kill someone.

"Lady, this card is no good."

I was in Four-bucks. The gum-chewing barista held out the credit card. The one with my name on it. My real name.

"What?"

She shrugged. "Machine says it's been 'compromised.'" She struggled over that big word.

"You're kidding me." I snatched it from her hand. Then I stared at it to make sure I had given her the right one. Bugger. It was. I stormed out of the store without my double cream-no sugar and pound of beans.

Outside in the sunlight, I punched a number on my cell.

"Where are you?" I said to Sammy.

"At the chicken coop."

"I'll be there in fifteen," I said. I clicked the phone off and went to find my car.

Sammy is the underboss and Jewish cousin of my godfather, Uncle Vince. Yes, we can buy both bagels and bologna wholesale in this family. He's a little guy, short on muscle but long on brains.

I drove along Barton and turned left.

We have a chicken coop on the shores of Lake Ontario. This is one of several properties owned by the family in the industrial city of Hamilton. Our skyline includes steel plants. We consider smog a condiment.

The chicken coop is really a two-bedroom cottage. Some relative long ago kept chickens out back, so the place was assessed as a chicken coop for tax purposes. The chickens are long gone, but they never paid much tax anyway.

We use it for private meetings, if you get my drift. And warehousing. I try not to think about that.

I sped along North Service Road and swung onto a gravel drive. Sunlight glistened off Lake Ontario. Pretty, but it was November, and the water looked cold. I stopped the car and vaulted out.

Sammy's black Mercedes was parked farther up the drive. So was an expensive Italian motorcycle I recognized.

I flung open the flimsy wooden door and stormed into the cottage.

"Where's the son of a bitch? I'm gonna kill him!"

The place was dark inside. A single lightbulb hung from a wire in the center of the room. It took a few seconds for my eyes to adjust.

Sammy was sitting at a small wooden table. Even in the dim light, he looked a lot like Woody Allen.

He looked up. "What son of a bitch, Gina?"

"Mario! He stole my credit card number *again!*"

"Whoops." My dopey cousin Mario was sitting opposite Sammy, in the dark corner. He rocked back on the wooden chair.

I marched over and swatted his dark curly head.

"Ouch!" Mario ducked too late. His hands went up to protect his good-looking face.

"Second time this month! I have to get a new card AGAIN." I was steaming. "Someday, you are going to die cleaning your rifle, Mario!"

This was a well-known family expression meaning something entirely different. But the result was the same.

Sammy folded his arms across his scrawny chest and tch-tched.

"Mario, you careless nincompoop. You gotta check those numbers against names in the family before you reissue a phony card."

"Sorry, Uncle Sammy."

"Don't cut corners. This whole business depends on doing it right the first time." He waggled a finger. "Take it up a level. How would we ever get ahead if we just kept stealing from family members?"

"Won't do it again, Gina," Mario promised. He sounded morose.

I was still miffed. WHY did I have to be born to this family in this burg? Why couldn't I be from a little farm town in the American Midwest or something, where people actually did raise chickens?

Credit-card theft was so lowbrow.

"Why are we still doing this anyway? Isn't this rinky-dink?"

Sammy shrugged. "Hard times, Gina. Gotta train the youngsters on the little shit before we move them on to—"

"Stop right there!" I slapped my hand to my forehead. "Just forget I said that. I don't want to know."

Sammy smiled. It was a little creepy. He stuck a hand in his pocket.

"Sorry for the inconvenience, sweetheart. Here's some recompense for all your trouble. Go buy yourself something nice."

Melodie Campbell

He handed me a bunch of fives. A whole bunch. Probably a hundred. They came with a nice paper band wrapped around them.

I was immediately suspicious.

"Something tells me these weren't printed by our government."

He shrugged.

"Fives? We're doing fives now?" I blurted.

"We're not doing anything, doll." Sammy smiled. "We're merely in the import business."

I was confused. What were we importing? I looked down at the bundle in my hand.

"Holy shit. These are made in CHINA?"

"Watch the language! Miriam don't like it when you talk like that."

I paced the floor, flinging my arms.

"We're importing counterfeit Canadian bills from China now? Do we have to give away ALL our manufacturing in this country?"

Sammy looked apologetic. "Blame the politicians, sweetheart."

"This country is freaking nuts." I was peeved. I mean, really. We couldn't even produce our own fake currency now? Did all the paper mills burn down or something?

It was a disgrace.

"They do it a lot cheaper, doll. And they got the technology. Those new plastic twenties are harder to fake. We don't have the time or the know-how to keep up. So I got this connection in Canton—"

"Kill it. I don't want to know."

"—they make them over there and we launder them over here—"

"Of course you do. It's called *laundering money*." Jeesh. Like I wouldn't know that.

"No, I mean we really launder them. Through the washing machine. It makes them look not so new."

I stared at Sammy. Now I had a vision of Aunt Miriam standing over the Maytag, stuffing five-dollar bills into jean pockets.

"Of course, you have to be careful not to launder them too much, 'cause the ink they use over there isn't as good as the stuff we get here."

Mario nodded. "Runs more."

"This family is freaking nuts," I muttered. Not to mention unpatriotic. Giving away our counterfeiting business to foreigners. What else will they think of outsourcing?

"It's really rather clever. You should see what we import them in."

I slapped both hands over my ears. "LEAVING NOW. Can't hear you."

I stomped out of the place. Then I stopped to look at the sparkling lake to calm down.

Sammy's voice carried from the chicken coop. "Don't mind her, Mario. She gets emotional these days. It's the wedding."

I turned around and stomped back inside.

"The family is *not* paying for my wedding in counterfeit money!"

Sammy twisted around in the wooden chair. "Of course not, doll. Your godfather is classier than that. Nobody pays for weddings with five-dollar bills."

That made a lot of sense. But his voice was too smooth. I left there feeling vaguely unsettled, and vowed to keep an eye on things.

* * *

When I got home, I threw the packet of bills on the counter. Why had I even taken them? Force of habit, I guessed. A habit I was determined to kick.

I shrugged out of my all-purpose red leather jacket.

The phone was ringing. I picked it up.

"Hey, beautiful. What's happening?" It was Pete, my fiancé. He's a sports reporter for our local paper, the *Steeltown Star*. He's also six foot two and built like a football star. Which he was, until recently.

I felt warm all over. "Same ol', same ol'," I said. This was the truth, if you didn't count the tiny matter of counterfeit bills from China. Pete didn't need to know about that. He wasn't part of the family yet. Wouldn't be until we were married. In fact, he thought I had gone completely straight.

Which was sort of true. I wanted to. I was trying to.

It was harder than you'd think. I decided to ignore the packet of counterfeit fives on the counter.

"Want me to come over for dinner?"

I grinned. "Are you putting yourself on the menu?"

He laughed. God, I loved how he laughed.

"I was thinking the other way around. Shall I bring Chinese takeout?"

I gulped. What was it about that country today?

"Sure," I said. "And don't forget the fortune cookies." I needed to hear some good news.

TWO

I may have mentioned this before, but someday I am going to write a book. It will be called *Burglary for Dummies* and will have all sorts of helpful hints in it, like "Don't risk your butt for a fake."

My family is very into fakes. Me, not so much anymore. That would be because my ratface cousin Carmine tried to pull one over on me a while back. It's not nice to switch real gems with fakes in your cousin's store. All sorts of people get upset, especially certain family members. They may even try to arrange for you to get shot while cleaning your rifle...but I digress.

Okay, here's the family position regarding fakes. Does anybody really get hurt? So your Picasso is not by Picasso. It's still just as pretty, right? So why the big deal?

I don't necessarily agree with this, by the way. I'm merely relaying the family opinion.

Sammy called at ten the next morning. "Got bad news, sweetheart. Your great-uncle Seb had a massive heart attack last night. He's alive, but it doesn't look good."

"Aw, gee. That's awful. I'm so sorry." I was too. Great-Uncle Seb was a loner. He had a reputation for pulling really bad practical jokes. So not everyone liked him.

But I was fond of him. He was an artist. A really good artist. So good he could do Picasso better than Picasso, if you get my drift. "How did it happen?"

"He got this new model at the studio. I think that had something to do with it."

"How? She gave him a hard time?" That didn't sound likely. Seb was a weird little guy but totally harmless.

"Nah. I think it was more she dropped her robe, and he dropped from too much appreciation."

A coitus coronary? That sucked. "Poor guy," I murmured.

"I told him not to do nudes anymore. Not safe for a schmuck over seventy."

Bugger. Of all the rotten luck.

"So is he at St. Mary's?" I would go right over there, of course.

"Yeah, but there's something else."

I groaned. There was always something else. "Spill it," I said.

"I think you better hear this from the horse," he said. "Meet me at the chicken coop at five. And bring Nico."

"Okay. We'll visit the hospital first."

"Good for you, sweetheart. He'll like that."

We rang off.

First I called Tiff to manage the jewelry store for me. Tiff is my Goth-inspired shop assistant and Nico's little sister. Both of them are my cousins. Then I picked Nico up at his cute little condo on Caroline.

Nico is tall and thin. His shock-blond hair is definitely out of a bottle. But he's a sharp cookie, with a surprisingly check-ered past. Mainly break and enters, with a chaser of car theft. Never been caught. I love him to pieces.

He's gone clean, sort of. If you don't count the pile of burglaries we did together last month to get back those fake gemstones. The *Steeltown Star* called them the Lone Rearranger burglaries. But that's another story, and I prefer not to count those particular B & Es.

Nico is what you might call metro-sexual. That is, he doesn't exactly fit in with the lunch-box mentality of Hamilton, fondly called The Hammer. Maybe it's the eyeliner he's taken to wearing lately.

Today, he had dressed for the occasion. I mean, really.

"I didn't think black was appropriate since he isn't dead yet," Nico said, slipping into the passenger seat. "So I figured to cheer him up."

I looked over. Burgundy jeans with a wild pink, green and yellow shirt.

"Wait a sec—are those parrots?"

Nico grinned. "Do I rock the great-uncle or what?"

I moaned and shifted into Drive.

St. Mary's Hospital is right across the street from La Paloma, that posh Italian bistro on James. My uncle Vito owns it. It is also the family hangout.

I parked behind the restaurant. We planned to stop in there after visiting Seb.

The hospital itself is huge. It dates back to the time of cholera epidemics. My godfather is a major donor. There is even a wing named after him.

The behemoth of a building takes up an entire city block in the heart of downtown. Many wings have been added over the decades. The labyrinth of hallways is diabolical. The Emerg department specializes in gunshot and knife wounds. I had been there many times, to visit relatives.

Great-Uncle Seb was in the ICU, hooked up to a bunch of lines. He didn't seem to be awake. All sorts of machines were beeping around him. They wouldn't stop.

We walked into the room no problem. The nurses must have been on their coffee break.

"Should we wake him?" Nico asked.

I shook my head. "Let's just wait awhile and see if he opens his eyes."

Poor fellow looked awfully thin and gray...sort of...dead. That was it. He actually looked dead.

Rats. I'd seen dead bodies before (don't ask). This great-uncle was ex.

"Um...Gina?" Nico touched Seb's hand with his fingers. He pulled back his hand in a hurry. "Maybe we should leave."

"Yup," I said with a shake to my voice. "Poor guy needs his beauty sleep."

We tiptoed out of the room and down the hall to the elevator.

As soon as we hit the great outdoors, we speed-walked to the corner. Okay, we ran like freaked-out idiots.

Nico didn't speak until we were behind the restaurant.

"Poor Seb. Should we have stayed?"

I was feeling guilty too. "Probably we didn't need to leave. I mean, he did die of natural causes."

"We reacted on instinct," Nico said, nodding. "The way we were taught. Maybe he would be proud."

Rule number one in the Gallo-Ricci family is never be caught in the same room as a dead body. Except at a funeral.

"I'm not feeling like stopping at La Paloma. Do you mind?" Nico had clearly had enough of family for one morning.

"Fine by me," I said. "Let's go straight to the store."

* * *

The phone call came about an hour later, just as we were about to grab some lunch.

It was Sammy. "Change of plans. Seb poofed it."

"Aw gee, I'm sorry," I said into my cell phone. "He didn't look good when I saw him this morning."

No kidding. Dead is not a good look.

"Miriam will call you about the arrangements. I got a shitload of stuff to do now. Can't make the chicken coop. So let me explain."

He did. It wasn't as bad as I thought.

"Seb left me a painting?" This didn't sound like bad news. I loved Seb's original art and had told him so many times.

"Yeah. Nice one too. Not his…usual style."

"Well, that's nice. Something to remember him by. Do you have it?"

"Yeah. I'll drop it off at the store tomorrow. And sweetheart?"

Now I was suspicious. "Yes?"

"Seb was very fond of you. He was a good man. Remember that."

I clicked off wondering, What the poop?

THREE

The next day, I dressed in black for work, out of respect. Black pants and black scoop-neck sweater. I broke it up with a gold belt.

Nico was with me in the jewelry store. Usually, Tiff did that shift, but it was half-off day at the tattoo parlor. Tiff didn't like to miss a deal. So she got Nico to fill in for her.

Nico was also dressed in black, but that wasn't unusual. He often wore black. Right now he was leaning against the jewelry counter, paging through *Brides Magazine*.

"Tell me you aren't going to wear one of these baked-meringue wedding dresses, Gina. I'll kill myself."

I smiled. "Never fear. I'm not much for Cinderella froufrou. I'm more of the Grecian goddess type."

"Ooooh. Are you going for the Pippa look?" He frowned and flipped more pages.

"Huh?"

"Sister of Kate, the future Queen of England, silly. Remember the slinky dress Pippa Middleton wore at the Royal Wedding?"

"I'm too rounded for that, alas." It was true. To my dismay (and to Pete's delight), I was a Marilyn where it counted.

"Too bad there wasn't enough time to order a custom-made dress."

"No worries. Lainy is coming with me." And so was Aunt Miriam, Aunt Pinky, Aunt Vera and most of the female population west of the Red Hill Expressway.

24

I thought Nico was going to jump through the ceiling. "Tell me! New York? Milano? Are you picking it up in the States?"

I smiled. "Nope. We live in this burg. It pays to do business locally, if you can."

Sammy walked in the door. He had something big and square under his arm.

"Hey, sweetheart. How's things?"

I walked over and gave him a sideways hug.

"Hi, Uncle Sammy." Nico waved.

"Is that from Seb?" I tried to grab the parcel from him.

"Hold on, doll. It's heavy." He put it down on the glass counter.

I attacked the brown paper wrapping.

"Take it easy, Gina. It's worth a lot."

I grinned. Maybe it was worth a lot to me, for sentimental reasons. But Seb wasn't well known as an artist, for obvious reasons. His own work didn't command a price.

Underneath the brown paper was a painting about two by two and a half feet. The thing was framed in carved brown wood. It was a floating nude, with a bunch of other things in the sky. Quite colorful, with blues and greens.

"It's a Kugel copy." I gazed at it in awe. "Oh my God, it's the lady with the three—"

"He really wanted you to have it, Gina. He was quite insistent upon that."

We all stared at it. Nico twisted his head sideways.

"What's a Kugel?" said Nico.

"Kugel was from the same period as Chagall. A little later than Picasso," I explained.

Something hit me then. It didn't make me feel good. "I've seen this before."

Sammy squirmed. His face twisted.

"Recently," I said, thinking hard. "And I don't mean in Art History class." That had been years ago, in university.

"Not this one." Sammy shook his head. "Even I haven't seen this one before."

Now what did he mean by that?

"I don't know, Gina." Nico still had his head tilted. "Were you thinking for the shop? The colors are right, but the three boobies might turn off clients."

I snapped my fingers. "I know! It's hanging in the City Art Gallery. I noticed it the night I was there for that gala, when Tony got hit." Hoo boy. That was so not a good night. Except for Pete. That's when I got together with Pete.

"Man, it's a good copy," I said, putting my face right up to the painting. "Seb sure was a master, God rest his soul."

"He left something for you too, Nico," Sammy said.

Sammy was looking funny. Almost as if he wasn't sure how this would go down. My mind raced through the alternatives.

"Not—"

27

Nico gasped. "Pauly?"

Sammy nodded.

I groaned. "The insane parrot."

"Oh my God, Gina." He clapped his hands together. "That is so awesome. My own parrot. Think of how it will go down in the shop."

Nico had just finished his interior-design diploma and was about to set up a design business in the store next to mine. The family was fronting him. I had no doubt the shop would serve a purpose additional to what Nico had in mind. But why disillusion the poor lad?

"*Insane* parrot," I reminded him. "And are you telling me you are going to design the entire store around the colors of that bonkers bird?"

His brown eyes went wide. "A parrot motif! Brilliant, cuz. I was looking for a hook."

I just hoped Captain Hook wasn't still looking for his bird.

"The parrot is at the vet now. Luca will bring it over to your place when they release it." Sammy looked at his Rolex. "Gotta run. So I'll see you two at the visitation. Miriam will call with last-minute instructions."

"Sure." I was still staring at the painting.

"Wear black, Gina. You know Miriam's fussy about that. Gotta respect the dead an' all."

"I'll wear black. Nico will help me pick something appropriate."

"I mean for the visitation and the funeral. She said to wear two different outfits."

Nico was all grins. "Are we going shopping? I know this new place in Oakville—"

The door slammed shut.

Something else was bothering me. I stared at the painting.

"Nico, I don't get it. I've been to Seb's studio dozens of times, and I never saw this there."

29

Seb had lived at the studio. No, I mean, *really*. He had a one-bedroom apartment above the studio. It was in a converted space on James North.

Not too long ago, that area of town was notoriously seedy. We used to call it the "scenic crack-house area" of Hamilton. This, of course, made the rent quite cheap.

In the last decade, artists had moved in from Toronto and made the place trendy. The Hammer is just over one hour from Toronto, where the rents are sky-high.

Seb's studio actually predated the trendy phase. Probably it predated the hooker-and-crack-dealer phase.

Nico tilted his head to the other side. "Maybe he didn't think it was respectable, what with the three…"

I shook my head. "Nah. He had lots of nudes hanging around. That isn't it."

I was bothered, all right. I don't like things that don't make sense.

"So you think he had this in hiding? Why?"

Good question. Why would he hide a beautiful copy like this?

My stomach lurched up to my throat. I put the painting on the counter. Then I went diving around the corner for my loupe.

"Hold the painting under the light, Nico. I want to check something."

Nico did as told. I trained my loupe on a certain spot.

"Shit. It's not there." I said a few more bad words as I straightened.

"What's not there, Gina?" Nico carefully placed the painting face up on the counter.

"Seb always put a little sign on his copies. A secret mark. He showed me years ago."

Nico caught my excitement. "Let me guess. You can't find it? It isn't there?"

I shook my head, gulping down bile. "This painting is the real thing."

FOUR

"So...that means the one in the art gallery..."

"Is a fake. Crap."

We stood in silence for a moment.

"How much would it be worth, Gina?"

I sighed. "Not sure. Less than a Chagall, but probably still a lot. Why don't you look it up while I take another look, to be sure?"

Nico whipped out his smartphone.

Click click click click.

"Okay. Checking Wikipedia...no, here's a Google link that looks good. It says the last Kugel sold for over a million."

A million. Great-Uncle Seb had left me a hot painting that might be worth over a million? "I think my heart is going to stop," I said.

"Thing is, you have to keep it hidden, don't you? Or sell it on the black market?"

Visions of prison cells danced in my head.

"Of course, if you really don't want the problem, you could always burn it."

"Oh God, I couldn't do that," I said. "It's a real Kugel! Burning it would be a sin against humanity. I'd go to hell."

Like I wasn't already going there. I tried not to think about that.

Nico shrugged. "Then I really don't see that you have any choice. You just hide the thing away."

I had to agree. But I couldn't stop wondering, How did the fake get there in the first place?

"So what do you think happened, Nico? You think the one in the art gallery was painted by Seb? And somebody made a switch way back?"

He frowned. "Probably somebody donated the Kugel to the gallery. And maybe they had Seb paint a fake before the presentation. To replace it in their home. Maybe he made two copies."

"And then the fake ended up in the gallery instead of the real one. How he managed that, I don't know."

"'Cept he was really good, right? Maybe he couldn't part with the real. Or maybe he just wanted to see if he could fool the experts."

I threw myself down in a client chair and groaned. "That sounds more like it. Most of his work was for private clients. He'd get a kick out of seeing his work in the gallery."

My cell started chiming "Shut Up and Drive." It was Sammy.

"There's been a new development. I've been talking to Paulo about the will."

My cousin Paulo is now a hotshot lawyer.

"Seb left you some money too. Real stuff, in the bank," he said.

"He did?" I was touched. Money was nice. Even better than a painting. I could actually use money. I wouldn't even have to hide it.

"Thing is, there's a catch."

I stiffened. There was always a catch in this family. WHY did there always have to be a catch?

Sammy continued. "It's about the painting. Odd as it may seem, the old guy was developing a conscience. You wouldn't think it to look at him."

Now I was on my feet. "Oh no. Not the painting. Not—"

"Paulo says there's a line on the brown paper on the back of the picture. Slit it. Look for an envelope or something. That should explain it."

The phone went dead.

"CRAP," I hollered. I reached for the painting and turned it over.

"What was that all about?" Nico asked.

I waved my right hand at him. "Hand me your knife."

I knew he would have one. All the men in our family carry folding knives. Some are bigger than others.

He opened it and handed it to me. I carefully slit the brown paper backing along the line. Then I handed the knife back to him.

"What are you doing?" Nico said, flicking the knife closed.

My two fingers just barely fit in the slit without ripping it. They grasped a single piece of paper.

"Seb left me a message." I carefully pulled out my fingers with the paper sandwiched between them.

My hand trembled. With a sick feeling, I flipped over the paper. The note was addressed to me. I read it out loud.

Dear Gina,

If you're reading this, I've already gone to that big social club in the sky.

I've left you my estate, with a condition. I need you to do something for me.

Put this painting back where it belongs. It's been bugging me. I promised Father O'Shaughnessy I would make it right.

You'll know what to do. You're the one with the brains.

When the painting is back, tell Paulo and Sammy. Then the money is yours.

I'm betting on you.

Love you, sweetheart. Take care of Nico and Tiffany.

Seb

The paper fell from my hand and drifted to the floor.

"Cool," was all Nico said. "His last practical joke."

I stared at the pretty blue walls of the shop.

I tried to focus on the stunning Murano glass sculptures on the shelves behind the counter.

Nothing worked to calm me down. So I picked up the phone and called Paulo. He answered on first ring.

I didn't bother with pleasantries. "How much is Seb's estate worth?" I said.

Paulo sighed. "Figured it would be you. Close to two mil, including the property."

Sweat gathered on my forehead.

"That son of a bitch," I muttered.

"You said it," Paulo said. He sounded amused. "Usually, you have to count your fingers after shaking hands with our relatives. But with Seb, you had to watch your back. Gotta run. See you and the Lone Rearranger at the visitation."

The phone went dead.

I glanced over at Nico, aka the Lone Rearranger. He was looking expectant.

"Hold on a sec," I muttered.

Something was bothering me. This wasn't the whole story, I was sure. Seb was trickier than that. I punched Sammy's number again.

"What happens if I don't do the job?"

"The whole wad goes to someone else. That is, if they manage to get the job done."

"WHO?"

He told me.

Very bad words came out of my mouth. More very bad words.

"Why? Why would he do that to me?"

"Seb had great faith in your brains, sugar. And he really wanted to put things right. He may have thought you would be a little reluctant to take on another job. So he provided an incentive."

I swore again. "One he knew would work, the son of a bitch."

"Hey. Watch the language, Gina. Ol' Seb is dead now, poor stiff."

"Yeah, and if he wasn't dead now, he soon would be. I'd be up for murder, not just theft."

"So you'll do it?" Sammy said.

My mind was whirling like a tornado. Was I going to let Carmine and Joey and Bertoni scoop my inheritance? Those losers? Joey and Bertoni had made my life hell in what Pete likes to call *The Great Shoe Fiasco*. Carmine had damn near ruined my reputation last month in the Lone Rearranger burglaries.

I would eat bugs before letting them get a single penny.

"I'll do it," I mumbled and hung up.

I'd break into the art gallery and do the deed or die trying. I'd break into freaking Fort Knox if it meant stopping Carmine from getting a cent of that boodle.

When I told Nico, he cluck-clucked. Then he tried to belay my doubts.

"Do you really think the cops care about stolen art? I read something about that once. Or maybe I saw it on television. Cops don't want to spend their time retrieving trinkets for rich guys who can afford to buy anything they want. They'd much rather track down murderers and rapists. I think it's quite noble of them, really."

"Of course you do," I said. "I'll remind you of that when they throw us in the slammer."

Nico chortled. "You're so funny, Gina."

More to the point, I was seriously nuts.

FIVE

The next morning, I had a lot of paperwork to do. I needed to get real work done before I could start to think about this latest development. At least, that's what I tried to tell myself. So I stayed at home in my condo while Tiff managed the store.

Aunt Miriam was the first to call. "The visitation for family is Friday night. Public visitation is Saturday. You don't have to go to that. We're holding back the funeral until Monday, so all the out-of-towners can fly in for it."

I swallowed. "The Sicilian connection?" We only saw them at funerals.

"Make sure you wear black." She hung up to continue the phone chain.

Around noon, my cell rang again. I answered without looking at the number.

"It's Pete." He didn't sound happy.

"Hi. Do you want to meet me for—?"

"Stop talking, Gina. Just listen." His voice was cold. "I'm at the police station. You're my one call."

Crap. "What the—?"

"Get your lawyer cousin over here. I'm going to need him."

Breathe, Gina! Breathe.

"What's the charge?" I said.

"Passing counterfeit money."

Crap, crap, crap. I started to hyperventilate.

I phoned Paulo. He answered in one ring.

Paulo would get him off, I had no qualms about that. The money looked old. He could have got it anywhere.

While I was waiting, I phoned Sammy on the burner phone.

"I'm off the grid," I said in almost a hiss. "Pete got busted passing the phonies."

"Heard about it," Sammy said. "Don't sweat it, Gina. We're moving it out of The Hammer."

I was storming. "Pete thinks I've gone straight!" Could this be more screwed up?

Silence. "Sweetheart, he ain't that dumb."

I hung up the phone. No, that's a lie. I threw it across the room.

Paulo got him out in less than an hour. They both arrived at my condo, looking grim. On Paulo, that's an unusual expression because he prides himself on looking drop-dead gorgeous. On Pete, it was more usual. At least, where my family was concerned.

"Why the hell did you get involved in this, Gina? You know better," Paulo said.

"I didn't do anything!" Paulo is my much older cousin. I always seem to revert to fourteen years old when he's around.

"Passing counterfeit fives." Paulo waved a hand through the air. "That's kid's play. Not worth it."

My mouth went dry.

Paulo shook his head. Not a hair fell out of place. "At least they were lousy copies. Even the cops could see that. When they tried to say it was family business, I pointed out we would never make anything so lousy. It was a matter of pride."

He made for the fridge and took out a bottle of water. "They bought it, of course."

Phew. I turned to Pete. "You picked those up where?"

Not that I didn't already know.

Pete hadn't said a word up until now. He just pointed to the counter.

"Crap," I said. "You weren't supposed to use those."

"I was out of cash," he said dryly. "I took two. Exactly two. For coffee."

"So I'm guessing here. Sammy?" Paulo leaned back against the counter and took a swig from the bottle. "The Canton connection?"

I nodded.

"Shit. I told him not to go offshore. *Everyone's doin' it*, he said. *Gotta get with the times*. I told him it was sloppy not to oversee your own operations." Paulo took another swig. "So how did they end up here?"

I decided to tell the truth. Paulo is a lawyer, after all. He has ways of getting you to fess up. "Mario stole my credit card number again, so Sammy threw me a wad as recompense."

"Mario stole your credit card?" Pete was puzzled.

"The number. It was a mistake," I grumbled.

"Shit. He's got to stop messing up like that," Paulo said. "Stole mine last month. He's becoming a liability."

"Mario's into identity theft?" Pete's voice again, more strident this time.

Pete and I looked at each other. He stood tall and broadshouldered and very pissed. His fair hair was somewhat disheveled. His face was hard. Damn. One look at that man always did something to my insides.

"I'm outta here." Paulo capped the water bottle and pointed to the door. "We never had this conversation."

We never do.

The door slammed shut.

Pete stared at me. I winced. His hazel eyes were usually warm and soft when they looked at me. Not at the moment.

"Burn it! I was going to burn it all," I explained, throwing my arms around.

He marched past me into the dining area and went directly to the liquor cabinet. This is usually a bad sign. He never marches past me without grabbing me for a hug.

He grabbed a bottle of single malt, opened it and chugged it straight from the bottle. Another bad sign.

I spent the next ten minutes explaining.

In the end, he was laughing. That's what I love about Pete (along with a thousand other things). He has a great sense of humor. All right, twisted. You have to be twisted to stay sane in this family.

"Let me get this straight. They're laundering money with counterfeit bills from China. But first, they launder the bills to make them look old. Did Sammy get them washed in a Chinese laundry?"

Okay, so that's what he was snickering about.

"Nuts, I know! Importing counterfeit bills from offshore. What is this country coming to? It's a disgrace, I tell you. A national disgrace." I had the nerve to smile.

He cocked his head. "So what do we do with this monopoly money now?"

This was a problem. No place to burn it here. We didn't have a fireplace. You couldn't stuff it down the condo toilet.

"I'll give it back to Sammy," I said. That made perfect sense. Or…I could hide it and give it later to someone I hated. I could think of a few.

At least Pete was mellow now. I decided to continue improving his mood. I plopped down beside him on the sofa.

"What would you say if I told you a poopload of money was coming to me?"

One eyebrow shot up. I snuggled closer to him.

"Real money?"

I swatted him on the thigh.

"Do I want to know where this is coming from?" Pete said, putting an arm around my shoulders.

"Seb left me something in his will." It was true, I reasoned. He'd left me a painting. With any luck, it would turn into money.

Pete smiled and pushed me down on the sofa. "I don't need money. I got pure gold right here."

That was the beginning of a really great lunch.

Sometime later, I thought about food. "You know what I'd really like right now? I'd like a big juicy hamburger."

Pete grunted.

"What would you like?" I asked.

"You." He put an arm around me.

I was feeling playful. "So what do you like best about me?"

"You're never boring," he said without hesitation.

"*That's* what you like best about me?" I sat up in a huff.

"Nope. Can't choose. I want the whole package."

He pulled me down again.

SIX

The visitation was held at La Dolce Vita Funeral Home. Yes, we own it. My cousin Enzo runs it.

"I've never understood the name of this place," said Nico, trudging along the sidewalk beside me. "Shouldn't it be The Sweet Afterlife?"

I grabbed for the door and entered ahead of him. "You think any of us are headed to heaven? In this family?"

He hesitated for a second, then kept up the pace. "You've got a point."

We went in the front entrance. Uncle Vince and most of my uncles would probably go in through the underground entrance at the back. Not all funeral homes have this, but the ones in our family do. Definitely handy for avoiding the media, cops and other disagreeable types who may have grudges.

La Dolce Vita is an Italian funeral home. Probably I should explain this. It has a big party room. Sort of like you would find at a wedding hall. Of course, they don't *call* it a party room, because that wouldn't be respectful. They call it the *friends and family* room.

The party room is decorated in what Nico likes to call *trashy Italian motif*. It's a tad overdone, what with the plaster columns and chubby cherubs. Souvenirs from the Coliseum in Rome may have more class.

The party room was already rocking. No stodgy music here. Seb had been a fan of the big bands. "In the Mood" was playing through the speakers.

"From what Sammy said, Seb was 'in the mood' when he had that heart attack," Nico whispered. He helped me take off my leather jacket.

I slapped his arm.

"Gina! *Bella, bella*!" Aunt Vera raced up to kiss me on the cheek. First right, then left.

Aunt Grizelda launched herself at me. Then we were surrounded by kissing, hugging, laughing relatives. Uncle Vito was there with Vera. Vince was talking to Paulo in the corner. Sammy and Miriam were in fine form. Pinky, Ben...the whole Steeltown contingent.

Pinky looked like a million bucks in a formfitting black sheath that had to be Versace. Even Aunt Vera and Miriam had new duds for their size-sixteen figures. They must have bought out every black outfit in

The Hammer. Because funerals are such solemn occasions in our family and all.

Pinky moved forward to wipe lipstick off my cheek with her thumb. "Heard Seb left you something in his will. Good for him. You go, girl."

When they finished with me, they moved on to Nico.

After the onslaught, Tiff shuffled over to my right. She had come with her parents. "I've never been to a visitation before."

"No?" I was surprised. We'd had a few over the years. Professional hazard.

Tiff was dressed as Winona Ryder in *Beetlejuice*. "Mom didn't think it was suitable for a young girl." She sounded disgusted.

"No kidding. They're much too morose." I watched Uncle Manny demonstrate how to do a cartwheel in the center of the floor.

Nico tch-tched.

"Where's Pete?" said Tiff. She has a thing for Pete, but keeps it under the wire. I just know the signs.

Pete had said he would come separately. I scanned the room. My eyes stopped at a bunch of men in the corner. Pete was standing with my cousins Luca, Anthony, Joey, young Tony and—

"Oh no." I groaned.

"What?" Nico squinted.

I pointed.

Yup, they were all there. Joey, Bertoni and—wait for it—that ratfaced weasel Carmine. And Pete was standing there, laughing with them. Like they were friends or something.

"Don't cause a scene, Gina," Nico warned.

"Who, me? But I'm so good at it."

"It's a funeral, Gina. Think of Seb," Nico called behind me.

Like Seb would care. Knowing him, he was already painting the angels in their birthday suits.

I marched over. By the time I reached the testosterone circle, all eyes were on me. I stared back.

Luca and Tony were my first cousins. I loved them to pieces. They looked suitably gorgeous, in that Italian-stallion way. The other guys were distant cousins. I was fine with keeping them distant.

"Gina." Joey nodded. "Nice dress." He stood a few inches taller than Pete's six foot two and had a good hundred pounds on him.

"Thanks," I said. "Seb always liked this one." He liked any dress that showed off curves, of course.

I didn't hate Joey. He was okay, in a "quiet thug" sort of way. At one time, he had a crush on me and tried to get Aunt Vera to set us up. Not happening. Even so, it's hard to hate a guy who thinks you're hot.

But I had no love for the other two bozos from the Bronx.

Bertoni looked suitably greasy for the occasion. I could do without him. Forever. Carmine the Weasel just sniffed. His face was as pointy as I remembered.

All three were in stark black suits. They looked uncomfortable, like penguins at a hot-tub party. Joey kept fingering the collar around his neck.

"You boys leave your heaters at the door?" I said. I practically growled it.

"Behave yourself." Pete whacked my butt. For some reason, the cousins liked Pete, and vice versa. This was one factor not in his favor.

"Big Sally couldn't make it," Joey said. "He was 'otherwise detained.'" Joey made quotation marks with his fingers.

I gasped. "The hospital or the clinker?"

"Neither. The wife caught him with a hooker."

Yikes!

Luca shook his head knowingly. "Will he live?"

"She wouldn't let him die. That's too easy," said Joey. "But he won't be popping the weasel anytime soon."

Bertoni shivered. Big Sally's wife was related to Aunt Miriam. Believe me, this was a whole new level of scary. You think the men in our family are dangerous...

"We're representing the New York branch," Carmine added. "On account of Seb being well regarded."

I raised an eyebrow. What had Seb been doing for Big Sally and the New York branch of the family?

"Heard you inherited a bundle," Joey said to me.

I turned my head to search his eyes. How much did Joey know about the terms of my inheritance? Did he know what would happen if I didn't come through?

I was about to respond with a question when heads turned. Abruptly, the boys were at attention. Vince? Nope. I had to grin.

"So which of you handsome men will buy me a drink?" Lainy McSwain sashayed up and hung an arm around Joey's shoulder. She didn't even have to reach up far. He blushed bright red.

Everyone in the western world has heard of her, of course. She's the Lainy in Lainy McSwain and the Lonesome Doves, the hottest new country group north of the Mexican border. She's also six feet tall, stacked like Dolly, and one hell of a nice gal.

Oh, and my best friend.

"Hi, Swainy," said Carmine, tongue-tied as usual when in her company.

Pete snorted.

"You behaving yourself, honey?" She directed this at Carmine, who nodded vigorously.

She pointed a long manicured fingernail at him. "No more funny business switching good rocks for bad, right?"

Carmine had turned into a bobblehead.

Lainy might make merry, but I was less likely to forgive him. Carmine the rat had nearly cooked my goose when he was babysitting my store a while back. It isn't nice to swindle my very best customers. I had a heck of a time getting back all the fake gems and replacing them with real ones before anyone noticed. (Hence the Lone Rearranger burglaries of last month.)

Then I had to go to New York and collect the real stones Carmine had taken from me. Aunt Miriam gave me a little help there, in her special way.

I'd recovered the stones. But Carmine would always be a weasel in my eyes. I had yet to dream up a really good plan for revenge.

Gee, I guess that sounds a tad vindictive.

Lainy was clad in a country-singer-meets-Morticia dream of a dress. Draped black jersey clung to every curve. It showed everything and nothing, if you get my drift. It really set off her big red hair. She turned to me.

"Hey, girlfriend," she said. "When are we hitting the stores for your wedding togs?"

I grinned. "How about Monday?" I said. "After the funeral."

"Yeah. Nothing like a funeral to put ya in the mood for shopping." Bertoni snickered.

I kicked him in the shins with my pointy Jimmy Choos.

"Fuck!" he yelled at the top of his lungs.

There was a collective gasp from every woman over forty in the room.

"Shit," said Carmine. His face went white. "Aunt Miriam is looking this way."

All of a sudden, my big, brave cousins melted into the crowd.

I immediately turned to Pete. "Why were you being friendly with that rat?"

I might as well have called my fiancé a traitor. That's what I was thinking anyway.

Pete smiled and shrugged. "They invited me to a poker game tonight. After this is over."

"A poker game. With that lot?" I stared at him, not convinced. He was up to something. I was sure of it.

"Hey, Gina." Sammy appeared at my side. "Miriam wants to see you about the funeral. In the crying room."

Of course, it's not really named the crying room. They call it the quiet room. Rarely, if ever, does it live up to its name.

While I made my way through the crowd, I stopped to corner Paulo.

"Does Joey know the conditions of my inheritance?" I asked him. I had his arm in a death grip.

Paulo has the whitest teeth money can buy. They were all visible in his smile. "Nah. Didn't want him to sabotage you."

That was a relief. I didn't need Joey's help. I was pretty darn good at sabotaging myself.

"Of course, he'll know if you don't pull it off." His smile turned crafty.

I had a sneaking suspicion Paulo was enjoying this. "Why?"

Paulo shrugged. "Joey will get to see the will. Then everyone will know."

SEVEN

At nine, Pete left to play cards with the cousins. Nico got a lift home with Tiff and Uncle Manny. I stayed behind with the aunts to help clean up. Which usually meant, to hear the gossip. For once, I tuned it out.

My job was to pack up the leftovers. All the while, I fretted and cursed.

What if I couldn't pull off the gallery job? Everybody in the family would find out. It would be humiliating. I'd have to move away. Change my name and skip the country. Maybe move to a small town in Tasmania or Bolivia.

Would Pete come? Damn. He had built his career as a sports columnist on his football fame. Pete had been a quarterback in the majors. His career had been cut short due to a catastrophic knee injury. But Pete had been a well-known quarterback with a sterling rep.

No, he wouldn't want to start over with a brand-new name in a backwater burg. Bugger. And I wasn't about to leave him behind. Guys like Pete didn't come along every day. Looked like we were staying in The Hammer.

Aunt Grizelda handed me a box of plastic wrap to bundle the leftovers. "You doing that heist for Uncle Seb, Gina? Good girl."

Jeesh, news travels fast in this burg.

"It's not really a heist," I said out loud, trying to convince myself. "Simply doing a teeny switch. Returning something that got out of place, so to speak. To its rightful place." I nodded several times. When you put it that way, it sounded almost noble.

She handed me a plate of cannoli and nodded. "Seb always felt guilty about that painting. Don't know why. He made a living forging, so why get all antsy over one painting? He was weird, that one."

This is true, I thought to myself. A Gallo with a conscience. What a novelty.

I handed her back the wrapped plate.

"Vince told me you had to return it or you don't get the money," she said. "That sounds more like Seb."

Sounds more like a Gallo too.

I could use that inheritance, what with getting married and all. Not only that, I could help out my cousins. Fund Nico to set up his store. Even send Tiff away to school to become a certified gemologist.

The last thing I wanted was the money going to Carmine and the Buffalo side of the family.

I just couldn't mess this up. And Bertoni and the gang knowing I couldn't manage a simple switch? I'd never live it down. Some things were more important than money.

I had to get this right.

* * *

That thought followed me all the way home. It haunted me well into the night.

When I woke up the next morning, Pete was sleeping beside me. He'd come in way later than me last night. It was Saturday morning, so he didn't have to work.

But I did, so I rose quietly from the bed and dressed. In black, of course.

The phone rang. It was Nico.

"Gina, can you come over here? I sort of need your help." His voice was shaky, and there was a terrible racket in the background.

Pete was awake now, waiting for me to explain the call.

"It's Nico," I said to Pete. "I have to run over to his place for a bit. See you after work."

I didn't wait for the response. Instead, I grabbed my purse and hoofed it out the door.

Nico lives in a cute little condo on Caroline. It's close to my jewelry shop in Hess Village. It's a trendy area of The Hammer, full of lawyers' offices, advertising firms and good restaurants.

The second I left the elevator, the problem made itself clear.

"Hoser, hoser, hoser. SQUAWK!"

Nico swung open the door before I could knock on it. He looked...frazzled.

"I don't think I can take much more, Gina. This parrot really is insane."

I nodded. "Poor thing."

The big bird was sitting on a perch in a large steel cage. You know how some parrots are pretty? This one looked like a punk parrot. Wild green feathers stuck out everywhere, and the eyes were crazy big.

I cooed to the thing. It gawked at me and then turned around on its perch.

"Parrots live for fifty, sixty years," I said. "They get really attached to their masters. Thing is, Seb went inside for three to five back in the late '90s. Pauly, the poor bird, was in grief. Probably thought Seb had died."

"Gina, that bird is mooning you."

Darned if it wasn't. *How* do you train a bird to do that? "That's amazing."

Nico groaned. "This isn't as much fun as I thought it would be. I can't get it to stop talking."

"Pauly did stop talking when Seb went inside," I explained. "I can't remember who looked after him. And then, when Seb got out and collected him, the bird went nuts."

"Probably thought it was seeing a ghost."

"It's a known fact, Nico. Parrots go insane if they're left by themselves. Just like people. I think the poor thing was neglected when Seb was in jail."

"So now..."

"Hey, baby, take it off. SQUAWK!"

"Shut up!" Nico yelled at Pauly.

"Hoser, hoser, hoser."

"It's simple, Nico," I said. "He won't talk if you put the cover on his cage." I demonstrated.

It was suddenly quiet. Eerily quiet.

Nico sagged in relief. "Thank God. I always thought I was an animal lover, Gina. But this..."

"That's not an animal. That's a demon bird from hell," I said. I flopped down on the black leather sofa.

"Want an espresso?" Nico offered.

I shook my head. "We need to talk about the painting. I was thinking about cleaning companies."

Nico smiled. An odd reaction, but then he said, "I already checked. We don't have the contract."

"Drat." Maids-a-Go-Go was one of the family businesses. If only they had the cleaning contract for the art gallery. Nico and I had similar minds.

Oh well. Moving on...

"What about the security guards?" Nico piped up.

I snapped my fingers. "What's Stoner's number?"

Stoner was a mutual friend of ours. His black standard poodle, Toke (short for Toker), was the talk of the town, with its Mohawk haircut. Stoner was a bright lad with a bad habit. But more to the point, his father owned Stonehouse Security. They dealt in high-end home-security systems. Did they also handle security personnel?

Nico picked up the phone and called Stoner. They launched into conversation.

I waited and watched the parrot. It was trying to destroy the cover of the cage with its beak. Sort of creepy, watching that beak poke at the cover through the bars.

Nico covered the phone with his hand and addressed me. "Stoner says they don't have anything to do with the art gallery. They don't do anything that big."

I thought quickly. "Does he happen to know anyone who is an expert in this sort of thing?"

Nico repeated this to Stoner.

I watched a slow grin split Nico's face. He lifted his head and his eyes were twinkling. "Stoner knows the best."

"And that would be…"

"A friend of his father's. Formerly of CSIS."

Gulp. Okay, that would do, I thought. It might even be overkill. Ditch that last word.

Most people have heard of the CIA and MI6. Here in the great white north, we have little ol' CSIS, the Canadian Security Intelligence Service.

After Nico hung up, he explained. "John" from CSIS was an old army pal of Stoner's dad, apparently. He just happened to be "retired" and living in Burlington.

"Is his last name Doe?" I asked.

Nico smirked. "Stoner will make the connection and get back to us. I told him to make it quick."

EIGHT

We arranged to meet with John for lunch at La Paloma. I arrived early and went back into the kitchen to see Aunt Vera.

She dropped her wooden spoon and rushed over to kiss me.

"Morning, *bella*. Sammy tole me. That Seb. Ay-yi-yi. He made things difficult. All the time, he made things difficult." She shook her head. Vera was clearly not part of the Seb fan club.

I shrugged out of my all-purpose leather jacket.

"You going to do it, *cara mia*?" she asked.

I didn't pretend not to know. "I'm thinking of it," I said honestly. "I have to weigh the risks."

Aunt Vera nodded. Her two chins nodded too. She went back to the pot on the big commercial-size stove. "You're a good girl. You'll do your best."

"Nico here yet?" A plate of antipasto sat waiting for customers on the steel counter. I was a customer. I snuck an olive.

"Nope. That boy is a worry. Why he care about draperies? What man care about draperies?" She threw up her hands in an age-old gesture.

"Nico's all right," I said. "He actually has a gift." I popped another olive into my mouth.

"You watch out for that boy." Vera raised the wooden spoon out of the pot and took a lick. "He listens to you."

I sighed. Great. Once again, I was expected to be the good influence.

God help us all.

When I returned to the dining room, Nico was having an animated discussion with the man seated across from him. I hurried over to the table.

The stranger rose to greet me.

"I'm John," he said, reaching out a hand. I took it and introduced myself. We sat down, and I struggled with first impressions.

I don't know what I was expecting from a former CSIS operative. This man certainly wasn't James Bond.

He was about average height and a tad on the heavy side. Not handsome but nice-looking. His brown hair was going to gray. His eyes took me in with one glance. He seemed to like what he saw. A thin smile lit his face.

Quite abruptly, it hit me. This was everyman. John would fit into a crowd and not stand out. Perhaps that had made him good at his job. And he had been good at his job, I was sure of that. There was just something about him. All his movements were careful and deliberate. It made you feel he could take care of himself in a bad situation.

"It's really good of you to meet with us," I said once we had settled. "I need to know about art-gallery security."

John lifted one eyebrow. That was it. One eyebrow.

It did the trick.

"We're not planning a heist," Nico said quickly. "We're not stealing anything."

"It's more like..." I hesitated. How far could I go with the truth? This guy was a stranger. "Let's just say the art gallery is missing something of value. And they don't even know it."

I met his eyes. They were a steely gray, but I could see a dash of humor in them.

"What do you want to know?" was all he said.

"Let's start with…what kind of security systems do they usually have in place?"

He leaned back in the chair. "CCT cameras. Probably motion sensors. Most do."

I felt my heart fall. How could Nico and I get around those?

"How old is the gallery in question?" John asked.

"1970s," I said. "It's one of those monuments to the god of concrete. Parts of it were renovated about ten years ago, I think."

"The alarm system may be original," he said. "Probably was state-of-the-art when installed. Most don't get updated like they should, especially the nonprofit sites. Easy to tell."

Nico shot to alert. "How?"

John shrugged. "Take a walkabout. Look for wires along the floor. Check to see if they are painted over. That will signal a system that has been there a long time. It may not even be working."

Made sense. "But what about the CCT cameras?"

John cocked his head. "They probably link back to a monitor in a security room. At least, that's what most people think. Television paints us a nice picture, but reality is quite different. There may be only one guard on duty. Those poor sods are paid minimum wage. How diligent are they going to be about watching every camera, every minute of their shift?"

Good point, I thought. Not to mention, if they only made minimum wage, they might also be working two jobs.

"Probably they have other things to do. Make the rounds. Visit the loo. Have a nap." John appeared to be reading my mind.

"How would you get past the motion sensors?" I asked.

"That's the tricky part. Those sensors can be really sensitive. For instance, a cat let loose in the building can trip them. And trip them. And trip them."

For a second, I just watched his face. It changed from impassive to tricky. One might also say...playful.

"The old 'crying wolf in the art gallery' trick," said Nico, getting excited. "Oh really, that's brilliant."

"The security guard goes to check when the first alarm goes off. And the second. But eventually gets fed up," I said. "I like it."

My mind was already devising a plan. How could we get into the gallery after dark? Or maybe...we'd go in at the end of the day and hide. Wait for the gallery to close. We'd have to bring a cat in with us, maybe in a bag. How would we keep the cat quiet? No, that wouldn't work...

"Of course, the easiest way would be to do the job when the motion sensors are off."

I straightened. "When do you mean?"

Now I got a genuine smile from him. "During the day, when the gallery is open."

Nico gasped. "With all sorts of people about? Isn't that brazen?"

John leaned forward. "The trick would be to create a diversion. A really big diversion."

My mind shifted to warp speed.

*   *   *

An hour later, the three of us had finished the pasta verde (best in the city). We said our thanks and goodbyes. I headed back to the store. I snuck into the back office while Tiff dealt with a customer out front.

A plan was buzzing in my head. It was the sort of plan that would require a specific kind of talent. Time to call in the big guns.

I picked up the phone and called Sammy.

"How do I get in touch with cousin Jimmy? You know, the old one who got

81

sent down for burglary. He's out of the clinker, right?" I was pretty sure there had been a party for him a couple of years ago. I'd probably skipped it—one of those phases when I was determined to throw off the family connection.

Like that worked.

"Jimmy the Cat? He's living at Holy Cannoli Retirement Villa now. But tonight is his pole-cat night, and he won't want to be disturbed."

"What are you talking about?" Jimmy didn't do jobs anymore. I knew that. His walker got in the way.

Sammy sighed. "You know your great-aunt Rita started that group—Speed Dating for Geezers? They meet the first Thursday of every month at the Bing-Bong Room. You know, the nightclub downtown that plays big-band music. Jimmy never misses."

"Speed Dating for Geezers??" First I'd heard of it.

"Yeah, well the real name is the Last Chance Club," Sammy said. "I just call it that. It's been a huge success. Who woulda guessed? Of course, they're all batty. Nobody can remember who they've been with before, so it's like the first time every night."

I choked. "A dating club for the nursing-home set?"

I tried to think of a bunch of old men and ladies getting tangled up with their walkers.

I shook my head. It wasn't working for me.

"Yeah, that little blue pill has a lot to answer for," said Sammy.

Now it *really* wasn't working for me. Holy cannoli, the thought of Last Chance wizened wieners…YIKES.

"Watcha want him for, doll?"

Okay, now it was time to fudge.

"I'm pretty sure I don't anymore," I said with a shiver. "The creep factor is out of hand."

Sammy was chuckling as I clicked off the phone.

Next, I called Nico. "I think we're in business." I explained what I needed him to do.

"No problem," said Nico. "I'll phone the retirement home. Jimmy and I are tight. He was my mentor before he went in."

I should have guessed.

"How many do you need for this?"

"Try for seven," I said. "I think the van holds ten. We both need a seat."

"I'll arrange the whole thing, Gina. Call you back." He rang off.

A short time later, the phone sang "Shut Up and Drive."

"All set," said Nico. "Here's what I arranged."

I listened for a while. Then he stopped talking, and I gave him the necessary details.

"Leave the bird at home," I said.

"No kidding. See you later."

Finally, I called Pete.

"Do you mind doing without me tonight? I have to help out with the Last Chance Club."

Silence. I could almost hear the gears in Pete's mind working. "Tell me this isn't anything to do with the family business."

Oh yeah. *Last Chance.* I got it.

I swallowed. Then laughed. I hoped it didn't sound too nervous. "It's a dating club for the retirement home. Speed dating for geezers."

"Speed dating for—"

"My great-aunt Rita runs it. None of the old dears have their licenses anymore. I offered to drive them to the Bing Bong Room tonight in the Cannot Hotel."

That was me, the Good Samaritan. It was a nice story. Hey, it was almost true.

"The Bing Bong Room. You're making this up." The words were scolding. But I could tell Pete was smiling.

"Am not! They play big-band music there once a week. It's kinda fun. We should go sometime." But not tonight.

Pete laughed. "Have to pass for now. Got a game. But you have a good time, babe."

Oh, I was going to have a brilliant time. Me and my seven heavy dates.

NINE

One thing about growing up in this family: you learn how to drive all sorts of vehicles. A lot of my godfather's businesses require moving merchandise around. Which is to say, we have a lot of trucks. I have access to most.

For this adventure, I picked a ten-seater van. It came with the optional upgrade to bulletproof glass, which I wasn't expecting to need on this occasion.

When I pulled into the retirement-home lane, they were already waiting. From the van window I caught sight of a sea of gray hair and walkers. A kindly male attendant stood by to help with the loading.

I shifted the van into Park and came out to greet them.

"Big outing for them," said the support worker. "Hope they don't cause you trouble."

Trouble? This bunch of elderly dears? I had to smile.

The attendant stood ready to help them board. I got back in the van to help the unsteady from my end. One by one, the Last Chance Club climbed aboard and found their way to seats.

"We're short a few birds," Jimmy announced as he shuffled by. "Rita can't make it. She twisted an ankle belly dancing."

"I warned her," said Mrs. Bari, who was right behind him. "*Rita, I says, you gotta lay off the pasta.*"

Great-Aunt Rita *was* sort of ample. The picture of her in a belly-dance costume was not doing a lot for me.

Mrs. Bari herself was thin and spry, like Jimmy. The usual gray curly hair came with an assortment of face wrinkles.

She sat herself down on a seat behind me. Jimmy plunked down beside her. This put him within conversation range. So I took the opportunity to ask Jimmy something I'd been wondering about all day.

"Okay, Jimmy. Why speed dating?"

"Sweetheart, it has to be fast. Not like we got a lot of time left or anything."

I sighed and took my seat. The support worker put the last of the walkers on board. I shifted the van into Drive.

On the way downtown, I stopped to pick up Nico. He had dressed up for the occasion. Black pants, white dinner jacket and spiffy bow tie.

"Channeling Sinatra tonight?" I said to him.

"Don't be silly, Gina. I'm Bogie." He fiddled with the tie and sat down in the tour-guide spot.

"Of course!" I grinned. "The Maltese Falcon. Or, in your case, Parrot."

He beamed a smile.

"Hi, Jimmy," he said. "Hi, ladies and gents. All ready for the big event?"

"I'm not a lady," cried one elderly voice. "And I can prove it."

"No!" I yelled. "Wally, do NOT remove your pants on this bus."

Luckily, I was driving. I had to keep my eyes on the road.

"Here. See? I'm a guy."

"Oops. Oh dear," said Nico. "I can see that."

"Can I see that?" said Mrs. Bari.

"PUT THAT AWAY," I yelled. "Nico, do something." I stopped at the red light. It turned green. I started up again.

Already I was getting bad vibes.

"Jimmy, are you sure we can we depend on them?" I asked.

"Were we supposed to wear Depends?" said one.

"I never wear Depends to speed dating. Takes too long to get out of."

"You don't go commando!"

Gasps all around.

"Gertrude, you always were loose," said one disapproving voice.

"The loosey bird gets the worm," said Gertrude, giggling.

Gack!

"Don't!" I said to Nico. "Don't even go there."

"How about we sing a song?" Nico said in a rush. "What would you all like to sing?"

"How about 'Barnacle Bill the Sailor'?" said Mrs. Bari.

"Ninety-nine bottles of beer on the wall, ninety-nine bottles of beer," started Nico frantically.

The chorus took over after that.

With relief, I finally pulled into the lane at the side of the art gallery.

"So we're all clear on the plan, everyone?"

Nico preened. "Yup. Gina will park the van. I'll lead the troops around and manufacture a good distraction. Jimmy can do his thing. We meet back here in twenty minutes. Piece of cake."

"Do we get cake?" Wally said.

We got them out of the van. One by one, with walkers and canes, they shuffled into the glass atrium of the art gallery.

As I watched them go, I felt strange. I wasn't used to waiting on the sidelines. But Nico figured I should stay out of sight. This was because of another incident that involved the police and the art gallery earlier this year. My second cousin Tony (meaning my distant cousin, not one of the other Tonys) had been shot by some guys from New York. Unfortunately, I had also been on the spot.

So Nico was supervising the actual heist, and I was driving the getaway car. At least, that's what we told Jimmy and the old dears. Best that they think this was a real job. It would bring back the good ol' days. Might as well give everyone a thrill since they were missing their speed-dating night.

When all bodies were clear, I steered the van into a disabled-parking spot in the parkade. Then I picked up my tablet and spent a little time reading.

Next thing I knew, Nico texted my cell phone. "All done. We're here."

I paid for parking and drove out to meet them in the lane.

We loaded the stealth seven on board. Walkers got folded and canes put to rest. I pulled away from the curb.

"How did it go?" I asked.

"You don't want to know," said Nico. He plopped down on the seat opposite me and groaned. "Really, you don't want to know."

"But I'm gonna tell her anyway," said Mrs. Bari. She was bouncing up and down on her seat.

"Put your seat belt on," I commanded. "Nico, can you get them all to sit down and buckle up?"

"My seat belt won't fit over my big—"

"Enough of that, Wally!" Nico sounded harsh—especially for Nico.

"Wow, Nico. What gives?" He was never short like this.

"Wally flashed them." Mrs. Bari giggled.

Nico groaned again. "That wasn't the sort of distraction I was planning on."

"Flashed who?"

"One elderly docent and the entire grade-eight art class from St. Bonaventure."

Oops.

"Everyone screamed," another old dear added excitedly. "Some even laughed."

"I did," said Mrs. Bari.

"They aren't even going to press char-
ges," said Jimmy.

"I had to promise that Uncle Vince
would make a big donation to the school
sports program," said Nico. His tone was
only slightly hysterical.

"But it worked," I said philosophically.
"All's well that ends well." Honestly, I
was relieved. The art gallery had the real
painting. I had the forgery. Nobody had
died. Nobody was even in jail. That made
the operation a success, in my books.

I was a happy camper. I wouldn't be
humiliated in front of the family after all. I
turned left out of the parking lot.

Nico opened the sack to look at the
painting.

Gasp. Cough. Mutter.

"What is it? Spit it out, Nico." Jeesh. I
didn't need all these dramatics.

"Uh, Gina? We have a problem."

"What?" I was already speeding down King.

"Um…really, I don't know how to tell you this."

"Tell me."

Nico sighed. "It's the wrong painting."

"WHAT?" I veered to the curb and slammed on the brakes. "Show me."

I slammed the transmission into Park.

Nico held up the painting.

"CRAP!" I screeched. "Crappity crap."

It was a really nice painting. She was quite beautiful, in fact. Rather Rubenesque, but in a good way. I could see why a man like Jimmy might like this painting.

But it wasn't the right one.

"Jimmy, I am speechless. Honestly, I don't know what to say." Nico's voice was starting to squeak.

"Whaddaya mean?" Jimmy said. "You tole me to steal dat." He pointed a bony finger at the lady's…unmentionables.

I held my breath for five seconds. Then I tried not to yell.

"Jimmy, what did I tell you to steal?" Nico said.

"The lady wit the big boobies."

I pounded my hand on the steering wheel. "No, Jimmy! The lady with the *three* boobies."

Silence.

"Oh fiddle, Gina. I think we had a communication failure." Nico shook his head.

"Jimmy, are you wearing your hearing aid?" I asked.

"Lost it," he mumbled. "Fell in the can."

Nico was moaning like he was in serious pain.

"Don't know what you're all upset about," Jimmy said. "I like this painting way better. Who needs three boobies? That's just weird."

Nico started to hyperventilate. "Oh my God, Gina. Do you suppose the art gallery will notice?"

"That their 'lady with the big boobies' is missing?" Of course they will. Could this get any worse?

"I mean, that they have TWO ladies with three boobies. Two of the same painting by Kugel. Don't forget what Jimmy was supposed to do."

CRAP. It got worse. "Jimmy, did you replace this painting with the one I gave you?"

He shuffled his feet, then nodded.

The fake Kugel was still hanging in the art gallery. And now the original Kugel was hanging in the same gallery, somewhere else. Plus, I had an original, priceless Old Masters painting on my hands. Recently stolen.

The gods hated me.

"Oh bloody hell. What are we going to DO?"

Nico pointed out that we couldn't do much of anything because the art gallery was now closed. "We can't do anything tonight, Gina. Chances are, no one will notice right away."

I tried to take deep breaths.

"And besides," said Nico, "we have to get all these seniors home. Most of them are already asleep."

I started the van to take the old dears home. But my mind was on other things.

How many days would it be before the cops showed up? I had to act fast.

TEN

I was alone in the store the next morning. It was Sunday, so we didn't open until noon. This gave me time to think.

And think I did. Plans rolled around in my head like a series of movie trailers. I considered some. Dismissed others immediately. It took a few hours to get the right one. Finally, the script was coming together. Individual players fell into roles. The whole moving picture became clear.

We would have to get this done fast, before the funeral the next day. And before the art gallery discovered the switch.

It was time to call in the troops.

Nico was my first call.

"I have a cunning plan," I said.

He listened without saying a word.

"Inspired," he said when I was done. "Really first-rate, Gina. Like an old-time movie."

"You'll pick up Jimmy?"

"Count on it."

"Don't forget the bird," I reminded him.

We hung up.

Next, I called Lainy.

"I need your help," I said. Then I explained.

"You got it, sugar," she said. "See you there at three."

Bingo! I had Lainy. The plan was a go.

Then I called Pete. This was trickier.

"I need your help," I said cautiously. Then I told him what I needed him to do.

"Are you going to explain why?" he asked.

"Em...probably you don't want to know."

Silence.

"This doesn't have anything to do with counterfeiting, right?"

"Nope. Not a thing," I said with relief. Forgery isn't the same as counterfeiting, right?

"No funny money from China?"

"China doesn't even come into it. I'm simply doing a favor for Great-Uncle Seb."

Pause.

"Seb is dead," said Pete. "Why's he asking for favors? Not to mention, how?"

This was getting squirrely. "Look, I'm sort of in a hurry. Can I tell you all about it after? Not over this phone. I'm not on a burner, see?"

Pete got it. And he agreed to do the deed. What a good man. I really did love this guy.

Next, I called Jimmy.

"Did Nico talk to you?" I said.

"Yeah. This time, we'll get it right. I got an accomplice casing the joint to find out the exact location of the target."

"Call me back with that info," I said. "Here's the plan."

He listened intently. Then he chortled and hung up.

Next, I called Tiff.

"Here's what I need you to do," I said. Then I told her.

"Cool," she said. "*Mission Impossible*. I'll get Stoner to help."

I could hear her texting as I hung up.

ELEVEN

It was nearly three when I arrived at the art gallery. A camera crew was just unpacking. While they gathered their equipment, I looked around for my accomplices in the atrium. It was tricky because the place was crowded.

Nico, check. Tiff, check. Jimmy caught my eye and winked. I could see Pete through the second-floor glass bannister, standing with his big arms crossed.

Toker the standard poodle was sitting patiently outside the gallery entrance. Good thing it wasn't a cold day for the poor beastie.

That meant Stoner was already inside. Check and check.

My heart started to pound. This could work, I told myself. It had freaking well better work, or I was out a small fortune. And, possibly, my freedom.

I dashed up the stairs to the great hall. The circus had already started.

Lainy was decked out in her western best. Red blouse straining at the buttons, suede skirt, cowboy boots and a million-dollar smile.

The art-gallery manager was standing beside all six feet of her. He looked like he had won the lottery.

Time to get this show rolling. I cried, "Oh. My. God. It's Lainy McSwain!"

Right on cue, Tiff and a dozen of her friends rushed up, squealing and giggling. They joined the crowd of at least twenty already around Lainy. She was happily signing autographs.

A good-looking young reporter man-aged to part the crowd to get through. A cameraman followed him, filming all the while.

The reporter stuck a mic in front of her. Lainy gave him a big smile.

"Thank y'all so much for this unex-pected welcome!" She just beamed at the gallery manager. "How did you know I was gonna be here? You sure are one smart fella. Handsome too. Ain't he handsome, gals?"

A cheer went up from the crowd.

"What brings you to Hamilton, Miss McSwain?"

Lainy turned to the camera. "I'm in town to help my gal-pal Gina hunt down a wedding dress. She already bagged the man. Now she's gotta git the duds. Ain't that a happy story?"

Laughter trilled through the crowd.

"Also, I'm here to get some inspiration for a new album I'm puttin' together. I like to come home every once in a while, Kyle. Grounds me."

I saw Nico sneak up behind me. He was carrying a large sack. Stoner was right behind him. He was also carrying a bag. Jimmy trailed them both, pushing a walker. It had a large sack balancing on the basket, and something else.

The first two shuffled up behind me. Jimmy carried right on through to the art gallery.

Usually, you are not supposed to carry big bags of things into the art gallery. They don't like it, for some reason.

But this didn't seem to matter right now, as all eyes were glued on Lainy across the room. The young security guard was transfixed, watching her every move. The ticket lady had come out of her kiosk.

The good-looking reporter said something funny. Lainy gave the gallery manager a big lipstick smack on the cheek.

Cell-phone cameras flashed. Lots of people giggled.

Pete snuck up beside me. He gestured to the cameraman and the reporter. "I called in a few favors at the paper. Pleased?"

I smiled. "Delirious."

I had my distraction. Now, just let the other stuff go according to plan...

People emptied out of the gallery rooms into the foyer, following the noise. At least, it was partly the noise. I had a backup plan going on, of course. And a backup to the backup plan sitting outside, if needed. Hopefully, Jimmy would keep everything straight at his end.

"Hey, Gina."

What the hell? My head swerved at the voice.

"Joey! What are you doing here?" Jeesh, that's just what I needed.

"Tiff called La Paloma. Said you needed people to show. I happened to be there, so Vera sent me."

I looked around. No Carmine or Bertoni that I could see.

"Where are the others?" I said.

Joey shrugged. "AWOL."

"Everyone says you're a shoo-in for a Country Music Award this year," said Kyle, the reporter.

"Why, aren't you sweet!" said Lainy. Her hips swung in time with her hair.

"What's your favorite song?" one girl called from the audience.

Lainy grabbed the hand mic. With a big smile, she addressed the girl.

"I'm partial to 'You Done Me Wrong, So I Done You In." But others seem to like my new one, 'You're Roadkill on My Highway of Life.'" She turned to Kyle. "What do you think, darlin'? Should I sing a few bars for these good people?"

"Sing 'Roadkill'!" yelled Joey. He started to clap and whoop.

The crowd went wild. Even the gallery manager clapped his hands. No kidding. Paintings by dead people never got this kind of press.

Lainy's big country voice swelled through the hall, clear and gorgeous.

"You ran me aroun'
So I'm runnin' ya down
You're roadkill
Stinkin' roadkill
On my highway of life…"

Someone whooped. The crowd went wild with clapping.

And that's when Stoner let the cat out of the bag.

TWELVE

No, really. He let a cat out of a bag.

At about the same time, Nico opened his sack.

SCREECH!

"What the hell was THAT?" Pete yelled beside me.

For one second, the room was eerily silent.

Then something flapped. It flapped again, big-time.

SQUAWK!

"Is that a pigeon?" said one of the girls.

"That was no pigeon," muttered Pete.

"It's a pterodactyl!" cried another girl.

"Don't be silly, Ang," said another. "This is an art gallery, not a zoo."

The black cat went to full alert. His back arched and his fur stood on end. Then he pounced.

"Fuck!" screamed Joey, who ducked just in time.

Pauly shot up to the ceiling. But there was nowhere for him to land, so he just hovered there, screeching and screeching.

"Who's a horny bird! Who's a horny bird! Squawk!"

"That bird just talked!" said the reporter. He was really excited. "Get the bird on tape, Randy!"

"Did that parrot just say what I think it did?" Pete asked.

It was the perfect distraction. More people raced from the back rooms to see what the commotion was about. But my

plan had a slight fault. I had failed to antici-
pate something.

"Back in a sec. Keep the cat away from
that bird!" I pleaded to Pete. It wasn't my
intention for Pauly to become cat food.

Pete whipped his gaze to me. "Was this
part of your plan?"

I put a finger to my lips, signaling sssh-
hhhh. Then I sashayed back to the shadows.

The cat hissed. It began stalking the
outer circle of the floor like a small feral
leopard. Then it leaped.

Tiff screamed. That set the tone for the
rest of the girls, who joined in.

"*Hoser, hoser, hoser! SQUAWK!*"
screeched Pauly, in response.

Now the bird was going mental. This
was not a good thing. Little known fact
(at least, I didn't know it): parrots, when
frightened, poop a lot.

"CRAP," yelled the gallery manager,
unable to avoid a direct hit.

"Crap! Crap! SQUAWK!"

Everyone scrambled. More girls screamed as Pauly flapped madly just above their heads. Iridescent green feathers floated to the ground.

I looked at my watch. Countdown *now*.

In ten seconds, I was through the double doors. Another twenty, and I was in the west gallery.

It kind of…didn't smell good in there. Evidence of the backup plan.

Jimmy had just taken the real Kugel off the wall. The one he had put there by mistake the last time we tried this.

"Hand me the one in the sack," he said.

I pulled the genuine "three boobies" painting out of the bag and passed it to him.

He got busy hanging it. "Now take that one down to Mad Magda."

"What?" I said.

"Mrs. Bari," explained Jimmy. "She's my accomplice."

114

I gasped. "Mrs. Bari is Mad Magda? *Our* Mrs. Bari?"

"Get goin', toots. She's waiting."

I picked up the other painting and ran.

No one was in the hallway. As I passed through it, I could hear yelling and screaming and, okay, cackling coming from the great hall.

Two turns and I was in the room where the twentieth-century paintings were displayed. Mad Magda—Mrs. Bari to me— had the other painting down when I got there.

"Hand me that," she said gruffly. Honestly, I don't think I've ever seen an elderly woman move so fast.

Mad Magda. Who'da thunk it? I used to hear tales of her pulling heists when I was a kid. Mad Magda was a legend in The Hammer. Watching her work, I could see why.

"Mrs. Bari, I've got to ask. Are you and Jimmy an item?"

She snorted. "We've been lovers for five decades."

Okay. Didn't really need to know that.

But I couldn't help thinking...was there a Mr. Bari?

She read my mind. "Mr. Bari died cleaning his rifle."

I nodded sympathetically.

"Take this back up to Jimmy." She gestured to the painting on the floor. "I'm going out the other way."

"Huh?" I said intelligently.

She gathered up her tools and sighed. "As part of the cleaning crew."

Ah! Clever.

"Nobody notices little old ladies," she said patiently. "People don't see past the gray hair and wrinkles. See you at the wedding."

I nodded my thanks. Then I picked up the fake Kugel and ran.

Jimmy was waiting for me in the "three boobies" room, holding open a green garbage bag. "Put it in here. I'll meet you on the other side."

I nodded and deposited the fake painting. Then I peeked into the hallway. Still empty.

In less than a minute, I was back in the great hall.

Things were calming down now. I saw Pete struggling with Nico to get Pauly into the bag. Joey and the cameraman had cornered the cat.

Lainy was still yakking with fans. The security guard was getting her autograph.

The gallery manager was wiping sweat from his brow. But he looked pretty happy.

Stoner was sitting against a wall with a dreamy smile on his face. In other words, being Stoner.

My eyes searched the room. Jimmy shuffled out from behind the...not sure where he came from. But he made the signal.

I backed away from the group to the shadows again.

Jimmy limped by with his walker. He passed me the green garbage bag, then continued on his way to the elevator.

I checked for staff. The manager, security guard and ticket taker were all over with Lainy, getting their pictures taken as planned. The coast was clear.

I signaled to Tiff. She turned and said something to her gang.

A few moments later, I walked nonchalantly down the stairs and out the front door, in the middle of a crowd of chattering girls. As soon as we parted, Tiff and the others started singing.

"Who...who...who let the cat in?"

All along the lane, they sang at the top of their lungs.

I grinned. Good ol' Tiff. Another distraction.

I snuck around the side of the building and peeked in the bag.

Happily, it was the right bag. Meaning, not the bag of stinky dog poo we had collected earlier. That was my backup plan for ensuring Jimmy could do the switch with no audience. Open a bag of doggy poo, and wait until people got out of the place. Then he could do the switch. Nothing clears a room faster than a bad smell. Who cared if they thought it was caused by a little old man who couldn't make it to the bathroom in time?

I smiled, remembering the bad smell in the west gallery. It had done the trick!

This bag smelled fine. I wiggled the plastic down the sides of the frame so I could double-check that it was the right painting. The lady with the three boobies. Phew! What a relief.

I took a second to breathe deep. We'd done it! We'd just pulled off the coolest switch in the history of The Hammer. Even better, I had fulfilled the terms of Great-Uncle Seb's will.

I turned around to check for Nico and smucked into a human wall.

THIRTEEN

"**I**'ll take that, Gina," Joey said. He easily wrenched the painting from my hands.

I stared at the big guy, in shock.

"What the hell are you doing?" I said, pushing hair out of my eyes.

"You get Seb's money. Seems only fair I get the picture."

"It isn't real," I said, shaking my head. "I already did the switch."

"It's real enough to fool a buyer," said Joey.

I stood for a moment with my mouth open. Then I shrugged. This could be good.

Joey could keep the fake and I would be rid of the...evidence.

"Knock yourself out then. I don't want it." I straightened. It was off my hands. Yay! He could do whatever he wanted with the thing.

"Do you want a parrot too?" A breathless Nico came up beside me. Lainy followed him, with Pete in her wake.

Nico was carrying a heavy cotton sack. It wiggled a lot. He had to fight with both hands to keep it closed.

"So help me God, if you bite me one more time, you are parrot stew!" Nico shrieked at the sack.

"Pauly want a quickie," the bag squawked.

"Gina, I can't take it anymore. I'm starting to channel John Cleese. OUCH!"

"We have to figure out how to reward that bird. It did a stellar job today," I reminded him. That parrot had just helped me earn a huge inheritance. And Nico didn't know it yet, but some of the money would be his.

"The rest of you did a super job too," I added. "I can't thank you enough."

"You can thank me by taking this sadistic parrot off my hands." Nico sounded frazzled.

"It's sad," said Lainy. Her voice had a lilt. "Poor thing is probably just lonely."

"Maybe he needs a lady bird," said Joey.

"I'll take the bird if you don't want it, Nico," Lainy offered. "I can use it in my road show."

"Lainy McSwain and the Lonesome Parrot?" quipped Pete.

"No, wait. Lainy, I just got an idea," said Nico. His face lit up with excitement. "We could run a contest to find a mate for the wretched thing. Think of the publicity. In fact, I've been thinking of this theme for my store, so if we shoot a promo there—"

While they were busy discussing parrot business, I walked a few steps away and called Sammy.

"Mission accomplished," I said into the phone. "I fulfilled the terms of the will."

"Good work, sugar. Ol' Seb would be proud. Just a sec."

I waited. I could hear Aunt Miriam's voice in the background.

Sammy came back on the line. "Sorry, gotta run. I have to get Paulo to bail your Bronx cousin out of the cop shop."

Holy cannoli. "Carmine? What did he do?"

"Apparently, he got caught passing funny fives. Imagine that."

The Canton counterfeits? I gulped. "Where'd he pick up something like that?"

Sammy chuckled. "At a poker game. You might want to have a talk with that man of yours. He has potential. Gotta run."

Potential?

The phone went *click*.

My eyes were wide as I swung around to Pete.

"You? You took those fives to the poker game?"

Pete was grinning.

"That's why you were playing nice with Carmine and Bertoni," I said. "I couldn't figure it out."

Pete's big arms reached forward to gather me up.

"Payback is sweet. Happy wedding gift, beautiful."

Payback, indeed. I met his eyes and smiled. "You are *really* going to fit into this family."

ACKNOWLEDGMENTS

Many thanks to my dear friend and colleague Alison Bruce, who loves this series and is always generous with support and encouragement.

Thanks also to Cathy Astolfo and Cheryl Freedman, who read my early drafts and provide feedback, usually in the form of laughter, thankfully.

Sincere thanks to John Thompson, for sharing his vast knowledge of security systems and patiently answering my novice questions.

And finally, I am particularly grateful to the wonderful team at Orca Books and particularly my editor, Ruth Linka, who makes every step of the publishing journey a pleasure.

Library Digest compared **MELODIE CAMPBELL** to Janet Evanovich. But comedy and mystery writing came to Melodie after she was a bank manager, marketing director and college instructor. Melodie has over two hundred publications, including one hundred comedy credits and forty short stories, and has won ten awards for short fiction. In 2014 Melodie won both the Derringer Award and the Arthur Ellis Award for *The Goddaughter's Revenge*. She is the executive director of Crime Writers of Canada and lives outside of Toronto, Ontario.

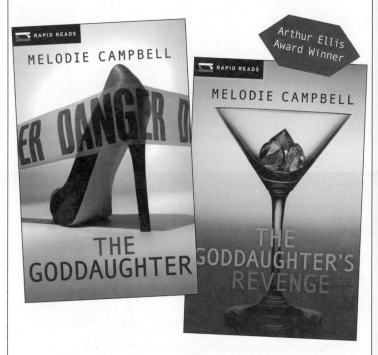